OLIVER
The Second-Largest
Living Thing on Earth

To my parents, the largest people in my life.
–J. C.

For my parents, Agata Y. Kim and Tony H. Kim.
–J. T. K.

Text copyright © 2018 Josh Crute
Illustrations copyright © 2018 John Taesoo Kim

First published in 2018 by Page Street Kids,
an imprint of
Page Street Publishing Co.
27 Congress Street, Suite 105
Salem, MA 01970
www.pagestreetpublishing.com

Distributed by Macmillan, sales in Canada by The Canadian Manda Group

18 19 20 21 22 CCO 5 4 3 2 1

ISBN-13: 978-1-62414-577-3
ISBN-10: 1-624-14577-9

CIP data for this book is available from the Library of Congress.

This book was typeset in Alice, Basecoat, and Chelsea Market Pro.
The illustrations were done digitally.

Printed and bound in China

Page Street Publishing uses only materials from suppliers who are committed to
responsible and sustainable forest management.

Page Street Publishing protects our planet by donating to nonprofits like
The Trustees, which focuses on local land conservation.

trustees

OLIVER
The Second-Largest
Living Thing on Earth

JOSH CRUTE

illustrated by

JOHN TAESOO KIM

PAGE
STREET
KiDS

This is SHERMAN.

He is the largest living thing on Earth,
and, boy, does he know it.

There is even a sign.

People come from all over the world to see Sherman. They take photos

and stretch their arms to see who can give him the biggest bear hug.

They crane their necks to see the top of his branches and sit on his roots to eat their lunch.

This is OLIVER.

He is the second-largest living thing on Earth,
but there isn't a sign for that.

Nobody hugs Oliver or takes his picture.

They pass beneath his boughs
without ever looking up.

He often feels invisible,

which is surprising
when you're 268.1 feet tall.

One day, when the crowds were swarming
especially loudly,

and the cameras were flashing
especially brightly,

and Oliver was feeling
especially lonely,

he got so tired of living in Sherman's shadow
that he decided to do something about it.

So he came up with
a plan.

He stretched his limbs
in winter.

He lifted logs
in spring.

He soaked up the sun
in summer.

He munched on mulch
in autumn.

By the end of the year,
Oliver was bigger and taller
than he'd ever been before.

But so was Sherman.

Oliver wilted.

He was still the second-largest living thing on Earth, with no admirers and no sign.

So he did the only thing he could think of.

He folded his branches, turned on his trunk, and looked the other way.

And that was when he noticed Agnes.

This is AGNES.

She is the third-largest living thing on Earth,
but there isn't a sign for that.

She often feels invisible, which is surprising
when you're 240.9 feet tall.

And this is GERTRUDE.

And this is PETER.

And this is GUADALUPE.

And this is LARS.

Oliver waved shyly.
He had never noticed them before.

This is OLIVER.

He is the second-largest living thing on Earth,
but he doesn't let that get under his bark anymore.

Because he is a part of something larger.

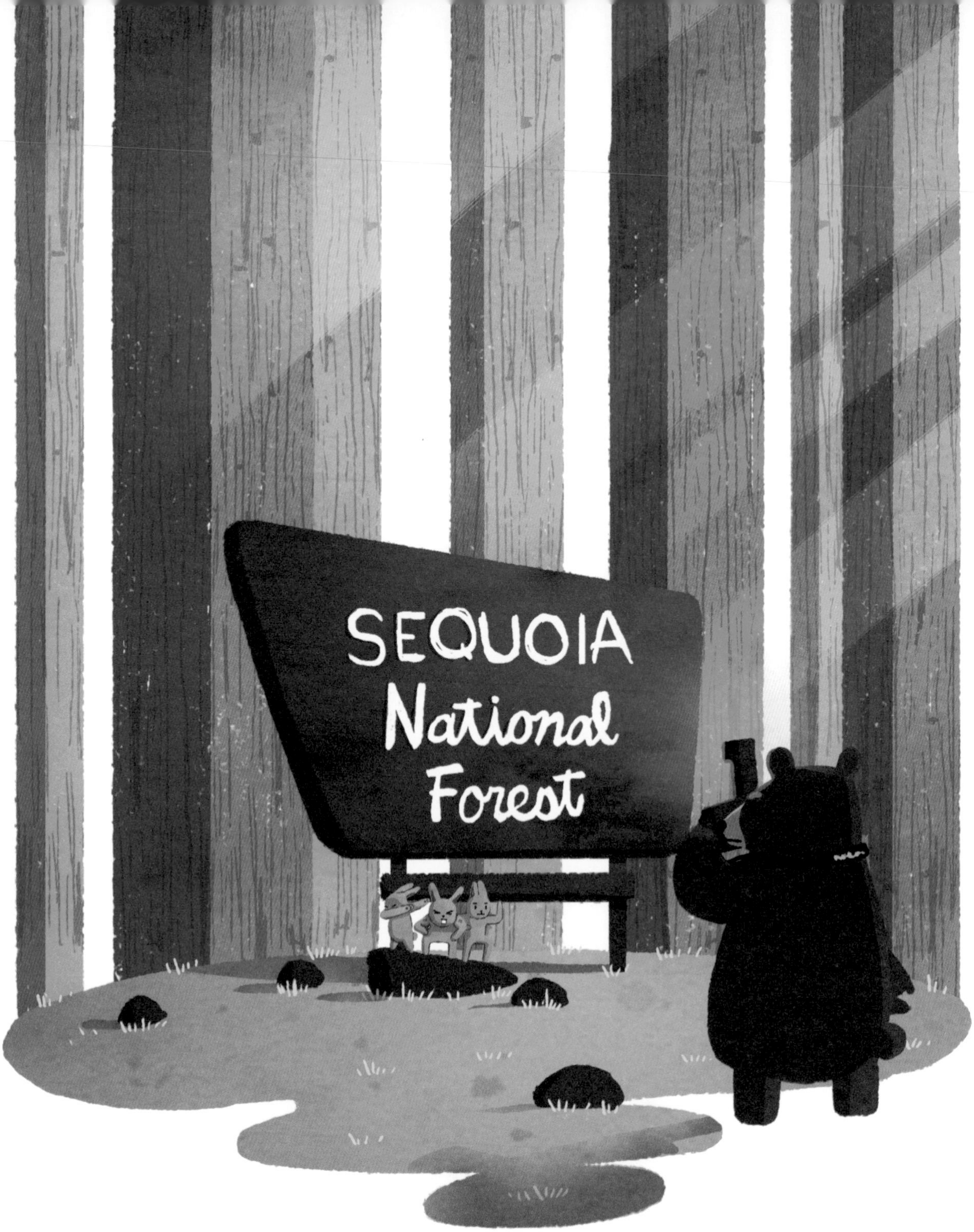
SEQUOIA
National
Forest

And there is even a sign.

THE REAL SEQUOIAS

While sequoias aren't the tallest trees in the world (that award goes to their distant cousin, the coastal redwood), they are the largest by volume, meaning they are thick and heavy—and perfect for bear hugs. The largest living sequoia tree on Earth is indeed named Sherman. The General Sherman Tree is 274.9 feet tall, has a volume of 52,508 cubic feet, and is still growing. The actual second-largest is the General Grant Tree (sorry, Oliver), which is 268.1 feet tall with a volume of 46,608 cubic feet. However, even Sherman isn't the largest organism on Earth: that would be the Humongous Fungus, a mushroom that covers over 2,000 acres in Oregon.

OTHER SECOND-LARGEST THINGS ON EARTH

For every largest thing on Earth, there's got to be a second-largest thing—just like Oliver. The second-largest U.S. National Park is the **Gates of the Arctic**, taking up 8,472,506 acres, while the largest one, Wrangell-St. Elias National Park, is 13,175,799 acres. Both parks are in Alaska, which is the largest U.S. state at 663,300 square miles. The second-largest U.S. state, **Texas**, is less than half that size, only 268,596 square miles.

The U.S.'s northern neighbor, **Canada**, is the second-largest country on Earth, spanning 3.855 million square miles. The distinction of the largest country goes to Russia, which is 6.602 million square miles.

South of Russia, in Nepal, you'll find the largest mountain on Earth, Mt. Everest, 29,029 feet tall. The second-largest mountain, **K2**, stands at 28,251 feet tall in Pakistan.

Water covers more of Earth than land, and the Pacific Ocean is the largest body of water, covering 62.46 million square miles. The second-largest, the **Atlantic Ocean**, spans only 41.1 million square miles.

Within the oceans lives the largest animal on Earth, the blue whale, which can be up to 105 feet long and weigh up to 200 tons. The **fin whale**, the second-largest animal on Earth, can grow to 89 feet long and weigh as much as 80 tons.